JONNY BRIGGS AND THE WHITBY WEEKEND

'Please look after Razzle and bring him back home with you tomorrow.'

Jonny Briggs and his family have gone to Whitby for the weekend and they're staying in a posh hotel for the first time.

It's very exciting and Jonny has put on his new black sandshoes and his special gold belt, but there's a small cloud on the horizon in the shape of a small, scruffy dog.

JONNY BRIGGS
and the
WHITBY WEEKEND

Joan Eadington

Illustrated by William Marshall

as told in Jackanory by
Bernard Holley

BBC/KNIGHT

© Joan Eadington 1979
First published by the British Broadcasting Corporation 1979

*This edition published 1985 by the British Broadcasting
Corporation/Knight Books*

British Library C.I.P.

Eadington, Joan
  Jonny Briggs and the Whitby weekend.
  I. Title   II. Marshall, William,
  823′.914[J]   PZ7

    ISBN 0–340–37187–0
        (0–563–20406–0) BBC

Printed and bound in Great Britain for the British
Broadcasting Corporation, 35 Marylebone High Street,
London W1M 4AA and Hodder and Stoughton
Paperbacks, a division of Hodder and Stoughton Ltd.,
Mill Road, Dunton Green, Sevenoaks, Kent (Editorial
Office: 47 Bedford Square, London, WC1 3DP) by
Cox & Wyman Ltd., Reading

1

The Friday before they all went to Whitby
seemed to Jonny to be one mad rush –
except that he was the one who hadn't been
doing any rushing until mam grabbed him.

When mam saw Jonny drifting home
from school at nearly teatime, she was on to
him like a load of bricks: "I told you to be
specially early back today, our Jonny! My
last words to you this morning were to get
back extra quickly for some money to get
your hair cut. You can't go to Whitby for
the weekend in that state!"

Jonny put his hand to his head. It felt
quite bristly and there was a lumpy bit
where one of the twins had stuck chewing
gum on it, during hymns.

His mother looked at him sharply: "Don't

let me see you scratching it, either. It shows it needs cutting!"

"I wasn't scratching it . . ." He stopped suddenly. With mam in one of her nattery, rushing moods, it was best to escape quickly. "O.K. then, mam. Give us the money and I'll go now. And I hope there isn't a queue of men wanting one hair each cut off. And tell Albert not to eat all the fish fingers if I'm not back!"

Mam gave him a fifty-pence piece and said: "And if the price has gone up again, come home and I'll cut it for you."

Jonny pretended not to hear the last bit. He prayed the price *wouldn't* have gone up. Even Humph – the calmest one – had torn up a school photograph of Albert and him with terrible fringes – all zig-zaggy – after mam had had a go.

Jonny had just got to the front door when Sandra came hurrying in from college. In a way she was Jonny's favourite sister – she never nagged at him, and all she ever thought about was cooking. And she was such a good speller she could spell words like *chilli con carne*, and *meringues*. Dad sometimes called her a walking dictionary with ginger hair, who could make ginger biscuits, ginger pudding and ginger beer, better than anyone else in Cleveland!

But now even Sandra was looking niggly. "I've forgotten to collect the sausage from the butcher's for the sausage rolls!" she gasped. Then she whispered to Jonny: "I'm supposed to be getting a whole lot of sausage rolls made tonight – so's you can take them on the train with you tomorrow, with a few left over for me and our Pat to eat while you're away. Mam'll explode if she thinks I've forgotten to collect them." She looked at Jonny pleadingly: "You could get them couldn't you? Be a good boy, and get them *before* you go in the barber's, otherwise the shop might be closed when you come out." Sandra gave him a big kiss and told him he was a pet – which he quite liked.

He ran down the road feeling all warm and good inside. He felt he wanted to start doing everyone good turns. He went straight to the butcher's – just as Sandra had told him – and collected the sausages. There were a lot of sausages.

Jonny watched as Mrs Stevens wrapped them up. He started to count all the slippery, pale pink links of sausage which Mrs Stevens twisted into sausages as she went along – almost as if she were making a long sausage necklace. There were twenty sausages.

Quickly, Mrs Stevens wrapped them up in greaseproof paper. Then, just as she had done that, one of her friends came in the shop and pushed right past Jonny: "Did you manage to get me that extra large ham and egg pie, Mildred? If you did, I'll take it right now, if you don't mind, because our Percy's just come over from Australia . . ." Yatter, yatter, yatter. . . .

Mrs Stevens became so engrossed with the story of Percy from Australia that she handed the sausages to Jonny almost like a robot. She never put any brown paper over the first, thin wrapping, or even put them in one of those small plastic bags.

At first Jonny didn't bother much. But as he went along the street he found that the sausages were beginning to burst out of the damp, thin greaseproof paper – and he had to try and keep wrapping them up again and tucking them up every few minutes.

And then, he noticed something else. . . .

There was a rumpled, roly-poly looking, scruffy, off-white dog with one black ear and a black-and-white tail following him.

8

Jonny groaned – that dog again!
Everyone said it was a stray that was kept
alive by bones from the butcher's and stale
biscuits from the bread shop. And now it
looked as if it meant to be kept alive by the
bulging, lolloping lump of sausage which
Jonny was trying to keep under control.

Jonny stood still in the middle of the
pavement, turned to the dog and pointed
his finger to the butcher's: "Go back!"

But as soon as he spoke the dog sat down
and looked at him. It cocked its head on
one side. Then it stood up again and
wagged the long, untidy black-and-white
tail, and gave a short joyous bark.

If I pretend it's not there, Jonny said to himself, it'll get fed up and disappear – especially when I get to the barber's. . . . And as soon as he reached Mr Clipper's barber's shop, he hurried inside quickly and shut the door after him.

What happened next is rather complicated. Mr Clipper went out of the room to get a sweeping brush and an elderly gentleman, who had been the last customer, went out and never bothered to close the door. So when Mr Clipper came back and shut the shop door, and grumbled about the draught, no one noticed that the dog had walked in and was sitting quietly by the chairs in a dark corner.

Mr Clipper had just started on Jonny's hair when he said: "What the heck've you got that parcel on your knees for, lad? Is it sausage? You should 'a' left it on't seats!" Then he looked across at the seats and said: "Oh – so that's it, is it? You brought the animal with you! And you'd no right! Dogs is never allowed in this shop under any condition. They's dirty, unhygienic animals, and if I'd have known before I started doing this cutting – you'd 'a' been out, double quick . . ."

"But *I* didn't let him in . . ." said Jonny. "He's not mine! He followed me."

"That's what they all say, laddy." Then, as he finished off Jonny's head with his clippers, he said, "Do you want anything on?" which meant he was offering Jonny the chance to have some green, gluey stuff rubbed all over his scalp.

"No thank you, Mr Clipper."

"Right you are then . . . That'll be fifty-two pence, please."

Jonny's face fell: "But I've only got fifty pence! Mam said . . ."

Mr Clipper glared at Jonny. "Oh aye . . . It's always the mams saying, isn't it lad? Well, tell her it's gone up two pence, next time you come. I'll let you off this time, but remember to tell her. And get that 'orrible animal out of here immediately."

Jonny hurried from the shop as quickly as he could – feeling all small and chilly round his neck as he felt a summer breeze wafting, like winter, round his ears.

Still clutching the sausages, he dashed home down Port Street. And behind him, in joyous friendly mood, dashed the dog . . .

"Thank heavens you got that sausage!" said Sandra, as Jonny dumped the parcel on the kitchen table.

"Thank goodness I didn't have to carry it any further, you mean!" gulped Jonny, who now felt his ears tingling and glowing from the heat of hurrying. "It nearly fell on the floor twice, and a stray dog –" He stopped as he began to wonder what had happened to it.

Then he forgot all about it because Sandra said he could help her with the sausage rolls. "But *do* try not to cover all the kitchen with flour," she said, as she unwrapped the parcel. Then she stared: "Sausage *meat*, our Jonny. Meat without skin, for sausage rolls! Well, we'll just have to squeeze it out like tubes of toothpaste into a bowl, and mind none drops on the floor for someone to break their necks on!" Jonny nodded, lovingly. He enjoyed making sausage rolls. He always liked cooking when Sandra was there, but it wasn't often he got the chance. Jonny helped her make two trays of neat sausage rolls with two little slits on each one for the steam to come out, and all painted with milk on top.

And when they were put in the oven, the smell was so good that Albert smelt them half-way down Port Street. "Can't we have some *now*?" he said, scowling, when he came in. "Why can't we? Fancy having all those sausage rolls and not eating them *now*! You're supposed to eat them when they're hot . . . you ask anyone. We can always get some more, tomorrow! So let's have them now!"

"Certainly not," said Sandra, as she took them out of the oven and put them on a wire tray to cool. "And if anyone pinches one – I shall never make another thing in this house! And I mean it! They're all to stay all nice – till mam gets back."

She had no sooner spoken than a strange sound began to well up through the warm air of the summer evening . . . It was coming from somewhere near the front door.

It was a strange, howling sound. . . .

Jonny's spirits sank . . . He knew immediately what it was. It was that dog howling. And it was probably howling because it could smell Sandra's sausage rolls – it was *that* sort of animal: the sort that never gives up where food is concerned.

Jonny went quite gloomy. He knew that neither mam or dad would like a dog anywhere near the house – ever since the day Albert brought back an Afghan hound from the park. Mam had found it taking up the whole of the front room and eating two chops which were supposed to be for dad; then an hour later a big car drew up outside, with a man who said Albert had enticed the dog away.

Then Jonny cheered up; at least this time it would be different. Tomorrow he'd be going to Whitby.

And he began to think about his swimming, again. He just hadn't *quite* managed it yet. But this weekend – he would really learn properly. Then he would be as good as Pam, and even better than the Brown brothers.

But that howling sound at the front door drew Albert towards it like magic. "I wonder if it's that big brown hound of mine that's come back again?" he said. "I'm good at training dogs, I am. That dog from the park never wanted to go in that man's car. It wanted to stay with me."

Then Jonny heard him shout (in a very disappointed, disgusted voice): "It's not that one! It's a mucky-looking thing! It's that one from the back of the butcher's that causes car crashes. It looks as if it's dying of starvation. It's howling because it never gets a square meal!"

At this, Sandra hurried to the front door followed slowly by Jonny, who was a bit suspicious of Albert. Jonny knew that according to Albert everything happening to other people or even to animals was what was happening to Albert . . . So that if Albert said the dog was starving, it meant that he, Albert was starving.

"That dog," said Sandra, "is a picture of health, and we don't want it hanging round here. It's a menace. We must get rid of it before mam gets back. There's enough to do without those things hanging round."

Just as she was speaking, the dog seemed to catch sight of Jonny standing behind Sandra and Albert, and it gave a yelp of joy and wagged its tail steadily. Then it ran towards him through the front door and into the hall passage.

Quickly Jonny turned away from it, but too late! As he went towards the kitchen, the dog had wriggled right past him and was leading the way – with its nose. Now it was Sandra's turn to howl as she suddenly realised the danger her sausage rolls were in. "Don't let it get them!" she yelled at Jonny. "Try and get rid of it through the back door. Do anything – *but get rid of it!*"

Jonny hurled himself forward in front of the dog and for a second he felt like a soldier hurling himself towards the ground in a fierce battle with a ruthless enemy. He wasn't a second too soon, and just managed to fling himself towards the kitchen table and stand squarely in front of the dog – barring its path towards its paradise of eating – as it stood there with its tail wagging with cheerful enthusiasm.

Jonny sighed with relief that he had reached the sausage rolls first, and shuddered slightly as he saw its glistening white teeth and lolling pink tongue – still hopefully ready to deal with the wire tray full of savoury goodness. He also noticed that he was alone. Albert had deserted him completely, and Sandra had stayed outside the door, not daring to watch a whole evening's special cooking about to be destroyed.

Swiftly, Jonny did the only thing he could think of. He took one of the sausage rolls and, holding it in front of the dog, coaxed the animal into the backyard.

It was an extremely difficult thing to do, and at first he was frightened that the dog

might jump at him and snap off his hand, and by the time he got into the yard near dad's cabbage patch he was sweating cobs! Then, quickly, he unfastened the backyard door and coaxed the dog into the back entry. Then, even more quickly, he hurled the sausage roll as far as he could – down the entry so that the dog chased after it. Then, with a gasp of relief, he rushed back into the yard as if a hundred giants were after him and closed the door!

Then he poured himself a mug of cold water and drank it all – almost in one gulp! Then Albert sidled into the kitchen followed by Sandra. "I hope it didn't breathe all over them," said she.

"Everything's under control," Jonny said.

And he felt extra pleased, because he had never said anything like that before.

Sandra put her arm round his shoulders and squeezed him affectionately. "Good for you!" she said. Then, her tone changed. "Have you *eaten* one of those sausage rolls our Jonny?"

Jonny shrugged away from her arm angrily. He could hardly believe his ears! She was saying it almost as if she was accusing him of stealing one! It just went to show that in the end Sandra was no better than the rest of them! All *she* had had to suffer was one of her precious sausage rolls being hurled down the back entry – to save the rest of them from certain ruin – and yet she was niggling over it. And even if it *hadn't* been used to save the rest of them . . . even if he, Jonny Briggs, had actually *helped* himself to it . . . to give him extra energy in coping with that dog . . . even then it would not have been much to ask as a reward!

"If he's had one I'm having one . . ." said Albert, as he nipped forward quickly and took the second one from the wire tray.

At first Sandra's face was like thunder and her ginger hair seemed to flame even more and almost stand on end with anger and desperation. Then suddenly she saw the funny side and said: "Well, seeing you've got one, Albert – I'll have one – seeing *I* baked them." And she and Albert started to really enjoy theirs, while Jonny, Jonny who had saved them and helped to make them, hadn't even had *one* for himself!

He walked towards the wire tray and started to take the third one.

"Hang on!" said Albert with his mouth bulging. "If he's having a second one I'm having one an' all!"

Quickly, before anyone could stop him, Jonny snatched at the sausage roll and began stuffing it hurriedly in his mouth. And at that very moment mam walked into the kitchen. All she could see was one person eating tomorrow's precious food – and that one person was Jonny.

Before he had the chance of a second bite, she took one quick step towards him and snatched the sausage roll out of his hand: "Oh no, you don't, my lad! If you think I'm going to come back into my own kitchen after rushing round for the past six hours non-stop to find you wolfing all that cooking of our Sandra's, you're *very* much mistaken. The best thing you can do is to get off, up those stairs to bed, double-quick before you feel a slipper across your backside. I'm just at the end of my tether." And she glared at him fiercely.

Then to Jonny's amazement, just as he was slinking dispiritedly from the kitchen, she popped the rest of *his* sausage roll into her mouth and said: "*Delicious*, Sandra love!"

Suddenly Jonny felt very tired, and he was quite glad to be going to bed. At least it would be peaceful and there would be no one nagging at him and blaming him for everything. And it was nice to be in bed first and have plenty of space to roll about or crouch up, even if he was still hungry after a mug of water and one small mouthful of sausage roll.

As he got undressed he began to think of tomorrow again and it cheered him up. I'll put my gold belt on, he said to himself, then perhaps I'll have some adventures.

He was just dozing off to sleep when he heard someone running along the back entry, whistling. Through the open bedroom window in the warm evening air wafted the comforting smell of fish and chips. And he heard the sound of someone undoing the back entry door. Then, drowsily, he heard a scuffle as Albert tried to grab some chips and Humph ran inside.

But the funny thing was, even though he was half-asleep, he was aware of something missing. And he was right. It was the door to the backyard. It had not been fastened again. And as Jonny finally fell fast asleep, a small, scruffy, white dog slipped back into the yard in the gathering dusk and curled itself up in a corner straight below his bedroom window.

And when they all got out, next morning very early, all loaded with suitcases and paper bags, and fishing nets, and cameras and sausage rolls and looking completely bog-eyed as if they hadn't had a proper night's rest . . . nobody . . . not even Jonny himself . . . realised they were being followed to the station by a small white dog.

2

"The Whitby line's one of the nicest there is," said dad as they all stood waiting for the train. He was wearing his cardigan that mam had knitted for him, his best trousers, and a new blue cotton cap with a peak on. "There's nothing better than catching the train to Whitby on a Saturday morning. Ten minutes out of Middlesbrough and into real countryside. You can't beat that!"

Mam was more concerned with the luggage, and keeping everyone together: "I want everyone here on this spot when that train comes," she said. "I don't want anyone getting lost or left behind. When you lot were babies your Granny got taken to Aberdeen through not standing with the rest of us – so just be warned."

Humph smiled good-naturedly and stood still next to her, and Jonny stood next to Humph staring down at his new black sand-shoes. He had put on his gold belt too – but no one said a word about that, and he was glad. He almost felt like singing – it was such a nice morning. Even the dusty platform seemed exciting in the sun. He hadn't been away for a weekend like this, for bed-and-breakfast, ever before.

Jonny gazed peacefully at all the other people waiting to get on the train: mothers and fathers with children, ladies in white shoes and flowered dresses, boys in Boro T-shirts, kids with buckets and spades. . . . He smiled blissfully. Then his smile slowly faded. . . .

Just as the train was beginning to draw up to the station platform, he noticed something that made his stomach give an uneasy lurch. There was a small scruffy thing trotting about the platform and mingling with the people waiting for the train. His heart sank as he saw it sniffing at a man's suitcase, then cheerfully inspecting a girl's sandals, a child's push-chair and a woman's green umbrella . . . and moving ever nearer to the Briggs family.

Jonny took a deep, disappointed breath. He had been hoping for a few adventures to start – but the sort of adventures that might happen if that dog was there couldn't possibly be pleasant ones.

As soon as the train stopped he hurried towards the carriage door to get in before the dog spotted him.

"All right, all right, lad!" called dad. "There's no need to go mad. The train won't go without us!"

Then dad made Jonny stand back again while he opened the door of a non-smoker for mam – to help her stop smoking – and helped her with the luggage.

Jonny was simmering with impatience now. He simply had to get on the train as quickly as possible. If that dog saw him he knew they would never get rid of it and *that*

would make mam natter all the way to Whitby. He could see the dog getting nearer to them every second. He could tell that black-and-white tail anywhere.

Hurriedly he pushed himself on to the train, squashed between Albert and Humph – feeling just like someone on the run from justice in a Saturday-morning film.

"Whatever's up?" scowled Albert, shaking his floppy black hair. "Why're you acting all strange? Have you seen one of the teachers?"

Jonny shook his head. The teachers never seemed to see him at all – unless it was straight after school and he was in a fight. He decided not to tell Albert he had seen the dog again. Albert was such a blab-mouth. And Humph didn't know anything about the dog in the first place – it would be too complicated to tell him. So he found a seat by the window and kept peering out to see if the dog was still there or had gone home. And this time he couldn't see a sign of it. As the train started off he began to feel more cheerful. Fancy bothering about that stupid animal on a day like this!

The train was a Pay Train where the coach has a gangway down the middle. No sooner had they got settled than Albert decided to look for the toilet. Mam nearly had a fit. "You're an absolute disgrace, Albert," she chuntered. "You can't sit still for two seconds at a time!"

In a few minutes the ticket man came round, and he was just getting the money off mam when Albert arrived back, grinning. Behind him was the dog. "Look what's followed me!" he said cheerfully.

Everyone – except Jonny – looked at him stonily.

Everyone – except Jonny and the ticket man. The ticket man looked at the dog and said: "You have to pay for dogs on trains . . . and he should be on a lead. . . ."

Dad looked up sharply from his crossword. "Dog?" he said. "Who said anything about dogs? We've got enough with kids – without any of those."

"Dogs?" said mam. "It's nothing to do with us. I've never seen it before in my life!" Then suddenly her face clouded over and she glared at Albert suspiciously. As for Jonny, he kept looking out of the window as if he didn't know what was going on. While Humph just sat there calmly and watched it all as if he was watching a play.

The ticket man stood there as if he was watching a play too. Then he turned to Albert: "Is it yours?" he said.

"No fear!" said Albert cheerfully. "I only like Afghan hounds. It was our Jonny that brought it home!"

Suddenly all eyes turned towards Jonny as he tried to shrink deeper into the corner seat, and he felt himself going a deep crimson. "I never – it followed me from the barber's!"

The ticket man began to look bored and started tapping his foot slightly: "Well, make up your minds. There's three courses open: it can be tipped out at Nunthorpe, handed in at Whitby police station, or it can be paid for and kept under proper control."

"But we can't just tip it out at Nunthorpe, it'd be lost," said Jonny. "It'd never be able to find its way back!"

"So it is yours then!" said the ticket man triumphantly.

"No, but I know whereabouts it lives. It lives behind the shops near the butcher's. We'll have to take it to Whitby with us and hand it in at the police station." Jonny looked round at everyone.

And as he said that pandemonium

broke loose and everyone started talking at once.

The ticket man demanded the dog's fare immediately – saying that they had accepted responsibility for its journey. Mam said she wouldn't be seen dead with it anywhere near her and that the weekend was going to be ruined. Albert asked what the Whitby police station was like and if they had any cells. Dad crumpled up his *Daily Mirror* and said it was all worse than being at work and if this was a holiday weekend the sooner it was over the better. Then he put his hand in his pocket and asked the ticket man how much the dog-ticket would cost. Then, with a face as grim as when the Boro had lost at home three times in a row, he paid up and said they would see about handing it in as a stray at the other end. And then Humph – the quietest of the lot – said: "And where is the dog anyway?" And at that moment they all suddenly stopped talking because it had completely vanished.

"What an absolute waste of hard-earned money!" said mam. "Well, I know this much, Jonny Briggs! Not one iced lolly or piece of candy-floss will you get from *me* this weekend. And if I see that dog anywhere near any members of our family again I shall leave you all and go and have bed-and-breakfast completely on my own with Rita in the caravan." She sighed, and shook her head at dad. "You must have been mad to buy a ticket for a vanishing dog which isn't even ours!"

And dad ignored her and smoothed out the paper to read again.

For the next hour everything was absolute gloom. The Briggs sat silently. Jonny was wondering if the dog would be waiting to follow them when they arrived at Whitby and whether he should ask dad if he could borrow the blue satin tie out of his case as a lead to keep it under proper control, like the ticket man had said . . .

Albert was planning how he would get rid of it for good by trapping it in the first butcher's shop he saw.

Humph was logically working out that if it tagged on to them again they could let it stay with Rita and Mavis in the caravan. They were always saying how they needed protection from all the dark, mad strangers with croaky voices.

Mam was brooding on the hopelessness of

trying to lead a civilised life with a stray
dog following them everywhere. And dad
was secretly hoping he wouldn't be spending
precious money on dog biscuits instead of
Brown Ale . . .

Then Jonny said aloud: "Just supposing
it does come back, and supposing it hasn't
got a proper home, and supposing it really
likes us and wants to stay with us. And
supposing it wasn't ever any trouble at all,
and was a good watch dog, and chased
burglars, and didn't eat much, and never
barked, and stayed in the yard at night . . .
And suppose I looked after it and gave it a
proper name, and fed it and gave it drinks
of water and gave it a bath every week . . ."

"Bath?" hooted Albert. "You never even
give yourself one, never mind a stray –"

"That will *do*, Albert," said mam in her
best voice, feeling like crawling under the
seat because Albert was giving such a bad
impression of their washing habits.

And so there was silence again.

But as the train got nearer to Whitby and
there was no sign of the dog, they all began
to perk up. And mam began to smile a bit
and gave everyone a sausage roll, and even
offered Jonny an apple.

And at last they were there – in Whitby
itself – with fresh sea breezes blowing
against their cheeks. As they walked out
of the station to the front entrance they
were greeted by the smell of the seaside and
the sounds of gulls screeching and
squawking in never-ending welcome. Sea-
gulls were everywhere, sailing away over
little red-tiled fishing cottages and swooping
about in the billowing blue-and-white sky
then, slowly circling downwards to perch on
chimney pots or stand like giant bird statues
on stone walls and jetties.

"Let's go down to the harbour and walk
along the part where all the boats are," said
Jonny excitedly.

"Let's go to that fish and chip shop – just
there," said Albert, pointing his finger in a
grand manner.

"Let's get rid of all this clutter before we do anything," said mam.

So they made their way to the Private Hotel where they were staying. It was up a steep hill, and had geraniums in the window boxes and lots of walking sticks in a big blue pot in the porch.

It was all so posh that Jonny was quite tongue-tied as they were shown to their bedrooms. Mam and dad were in one room, and he and Albert and Humph were in the other – all in single beds in a room as big as all three bedrooms at home rolled into one. And this bedroom had a wash-basin in it too, and a wardrobe and chest of drawers, and a chair each. And Jonny wished they could stay there for ever.

A bit later – when they met again down in the hall, mam said: "We'll go back into the town and have something to eat. And whilst we're doing that – we'll all decide what we're going to do next."

"Well, I don't know about you lot," said mam an hour later, as she patted her stomach slightly to try and press it in after a whopping meal, "but dad and I want to see what our Rita's up to in that caravan. Anyone else want to come with us?"

There was a heavy silence.

Then she said: "Well, if you're all going off on your own – make sure you stay together, and for goodness's sake don't let our Jonny get lost. Dad and I'll meet you at five o'clock – by that big arch made out of the Whale's Jawbone. And don't waste your money in the amusement arcades!"

When she'd gone, Humph said: "The tide's out, but I'm going down to the beach – anyone else coming?"

Albert shook his head: "I'm going to explore, across on the other side of the harbour. Dad said there used to be some old kippering sheds there where they used to smoke herrings so that they came out as kippers . . ."

Jonny looked at him in amazement. He'd always thought kippers were kippers.

"Then," said Albert, "I want to find that place where they make Lucky Ducks out of glass. And I want to find some real Whitby jet. *And* I want to count all those cobbley steps and climb up to the top of them and go round the ruined abbey and. . . ."

"Right!" said Humph. "We've got the message. See you at the Whale's Jawbone at five then."

The sand was all smooth and shining where the sea had just washed away from it. Humph and Jonny took off their shoes and ran out to the edge of the retreating tide of frothy white waves. Then Jonny dug his toes into the damp sand and watched as a thin wave of transparent water covered his feet. Then he picked up a small pebble and hurled it out to sea – just for the fun of it!

As he did so he heard an excited barking sound. . . . And there – further back from them along the tide's edge – splashed a small, white, scruffy-looking dog.

But that wasn't all. . . .

Jonny stared in horror at its one black ear and black-and-white tail – for now something else black had been added to it. And that something was one of Jonny's own sand-shoes which he had left on the beach. Now it was being tossed about by the dog who kept dropping it and barking and picking it up again and shaking it. Finally it dropped it again in the water, and barked and splashed, waiting expectantly for someone else to join in the game.

"What shall we do?" said Jonny gloomily to Humph. "If I go up to it and get my shoe it'll follow us for ever more. It must have sneaked off the train without being seen. But if I don't get my shoe back it'll mean even more trouble."

"I'll go and get the shoe," said Humph. "It doesn't know me. We'll just have to take a chance that it doesn't follow us." And he rushed across the beach to the dog. Then the dog leapt about even more with his shoe in its mouth, and Jonny saw Humph pick up a piece of driftwood and toss it in the air close to the dog. That did the trick. The dog chased after the piece of wood instead, while Humph snatched up the shoe and came dashing back to Jonny with it. Without daring to look round to see what the dog was doing, they both ran for their lives along the beach and mingled in with lots of other people.

"It won't be able to find us now," panted Humph as they both collapsed on the warm sand.

But for once he was wrong. Within a couple of minutes the dog was sitting next to them, wagging its tail. A large piece of driftwood was held proudly between its teeth. Humph smiled slightly: "It's quite clever," he said.

But Jonny wasn't smiling – he was almost

crying. "It's going to ruin our weekend," he
said. "Everyone will be nattering about it
and mam already blames me for it in the
first place. Just suppose it got into the place
where we're staying!"

Humph looked at Jonny, then he actually
patted the dog and smiled comfortingly: "I
got the impression that you quite liked it
when we were on the train. You were going
on about how you'd give it a bath every
week and keep it in our backyard . . ."

Jonny stared back at him: "It was
pretend. Everybody pretends some times.
Mam hates it."

"I think we should try and get it back to
its own home territory – even if we can't
keep it ourselves. It's no good just letting it
go on the razzle all round Whitby when it's

followed us all the way from Middlesbrough."

Jonny nodded. He didn't quite know what going on the razzle meant – except that mam and dad said it sometimes.

Sometimes mam would say: "The man from the fish-shop's gone off on the razzle again with that widow from number thirty-two."

"We could call it Razzle," said Jonny, suddenly.

"Call what razzle?" said Humph – then he cottoned on. "Oh . . . this animal you mean . . . Our scruffy but faithful follower. Yes, Razzle . . . it's a good name. We might as well call it something. But the point is, where do we go next with Razzle?"

Then Jonny suddenly remembered what Rita had once said at home when they were having tea one day. She had been talking about living in a luxury flat with her friend Mavis. "And we shall have one of those Borzoi hounds with long gold and white fur to guard us," she had said. "They have the most soft and beautiful eyes in the world. And they're so refined and elegant . . ."

But funnily, as Jonny and Humph sat there staring at Razzle the dog, their thoughts must have been exactly the same, because they both said at once: "What about Rita and Mavis's caravan?" Then they burst out laughing.

"What we could do," said Humph, "is to go to the caravan right now. It's only about twenty minutes' walk away. We'll take no notice of the dog, but if it follows us we'll try and get Rita and Mavis to look after it. We'll have to try and invent something very special about it on the way. You know as well as I do, our Jonny, that those two wouldn't look after just any old dog." Then Humph smiled again: "I've just had a brainwave! We could say it belongs to that Pop Star who's on at Scarborough – the one they said they'd seen when they sent us that post-card. And we could say that he'd asked if *they* could possibly look after it for him

and then take it back to his old Granny
who lives in Middlesbrough.''

Jonny looked puzzled: "But they
wouldn't believe us . . .''

Humph grinned: "They're so vain they'll
believe anything . . .''

"But mam and dad won't believe it! They
know all about the dog because of it being
on the train.''

"You leave it all to me," said Humph
cheerfully. "And anyway, if the dog doesn't
follow us again, all our problems will be
over without any plans at all.''

So they got up off the sand and made
their way to the caravan site where Rita
and Mavis were staying.

And as they walked a small, scruffy
animal followed them obediently. Humph
took pity on it and called in a shop and
bought it a packet of dog-biscuits. And
Jonny nodded when the man said, "Is it
your dog?" Then he asked: "What's its
name?"

"Razzle," said Jonny proudly. And just
to make sure, he looked at Humph. And
Humph nodded.

3

"I wonder how the others are going on?" said mam as she and dad huffed and puffed up the winding hill path to where the caravans were.

Dad grunted and stopped for a minute, and pretended to be admiring the view. "Forget 'em," he said. Then he bent down and picked a buttercup and held it under mam's chin to see if she liked butter, and they carried on up the hill.

When they got near the door of the big green caravan where Rita and Mavis were staying, Rita came out, and waved at them. Her face was covered in white cream and she had a towel round her head and before they could actually step inside she said: "I hope you won't be staying long because

Mavis and I are just getting ready to go out. We're going to a lecture about Count Dracula tonight with two people we met. Dracula came to Whitby on a sailing ship, and Mavis and I might join the Dracula society – if these two people. . . ."

"Dracula?" said mam, looking startled. "Dracula with those big fangs, that drinks blood! Rita, how could you?"

"Never mind Dracula and all that rubbish," said dad. "Just get that kettle on and be quick about it. And as for drinking blood – it was a pity he didn't have the sense to eat black puddings instead." Then he went inside and flopped down so hard on a seat that the van trembled, and Mavis – who also had a towel round her head and white cream all over her face – went all pink under the cream.

Then Rita said in quite a kind voice: "You both look worn out," which didn't really please mam at all because she was trying out some new Healthy Glow make-up foundation.

"Did you have a nice journey on the train then?" said Rita. "I must say I don't envy you – staying with our Jonny and the other two."

"We don't need your sympathy, Rita," said mam, as she sipped her tea. "The boys are behaving very well, thank you. And *they're* staying with *us*, if you don't mind." Then she added: "Except for that dog on the train that followed Jonny . . ."

"A DOG!" said Rita. "How awful!"

"Yes, and Dad was daft enough to buy it a ticket as well –"

"How awful!" said Rita again. "I don't know how you put up with them, mam." Then she began to get all restless and kept looking out of the caravan window, until finally, she said: "Well, you and dad are looking really fit now! That cup of tea has worked wonders. So hadn't you better be getting back?"

Mam hesitated as if she didn't really want to leave. Then she sighed slightly and said, "I expect we had better go, then, Rita. We've promised to meet the boys at five. Now, are you sure you're both getting enough to eat? And remember, don't let any strangers into the van no matter how nice they are. And as for Dracula. . . ." her voice faltered uneasily.

"Don't *worry*, mam," said Rita.

"No," said dad as they got up to leave,

"it's Dracula who'll have to worry if they're about."

"Phew . . ." said Rita thankfully as she saw dad's stout shape and mam's thinner one, disappearing from view. "I thought they'd stay for ever!"

Then she and Mavis both put on black dresses, and Rita wore a skull and crossbones brooch made from thick silver wire, and a hat with a black veil.

They were just going to lock the van door, when she saw the second lot of unwelcome visitors arriving, and she froze in horror. "Oh NO!" she said in a desperate voice. "Not *them* . . . here!"

"Hello Rita," said Humph cheerfully as he and Jonny and the dog stood facing the two girls: "We've brought you a guard dog to look after till tomorrow. It belongs to that Pop Star that you got to know in Scarborough. He wants you to look after it and take it back to Middlesbrough."

Rita nearly exploded. "What on earth are you *talking* about?" she yelled. "I never heard such a load of tripe!"

"It's true," said Jonny. "It belongs to that Pop Star you mentioned on the postcard you sent us, and he wants you to look after it. We met him on the beach . . ."

"You little liars!" shrieked Rita.

"And anyway," said Mavis helpfully, "Rita never even met him really – we just saw him walk past." Then Mavis put her hand over her mouth and looked all embarrassed.

"Don't alarm yourselves making up all that rubbish," said Rita. "That dog followed our Jonny on the train. It's nothing to do with Mavis and me – and we don't want it anywhere near us – so there!"

Then, without another word, she and Mavis hurried away and left them standing there. But as they went, Jonny noticed something. They had been in such a hurry that they'd left the caravan door unfastened.

Humph grinned at Jonny. Then, calmly, he opened the door and they both went in. Humph put some dog biscuits on a plate on the floor of the van, along with some water, and said: "We'll leave Razzle here to guard things for them, and we'll leave a note."

Then he found a pen and scrap of paper and wrote: *Please look after Razzle and bring him back home with you tomorrow.*

Then they hurried back to the town to meet the others at the Whale's Jawbone.

Later that night – at the Private Hotel –
when everyone had thoroughly enjoyed
themselves – and the lady with the frizzy
hair had made them a drink and put one
tea biscuit for each of them on a plate in
the television lounge, Dad said: "Well, I
reckon we've all had a very good day. All
that remains now is for you young 'uns to
get a good night's sleep. There's a fishing
contest on when the tide's in tomorrow, and
there'll be a chance for you to learn to swim
an' all, our Jonny – if the weather keeps
warm. So make the most of it, because we'll
be setting off back home again tomorrow
straight after tea."

Jonny smiled happily and dunked his tea
biscuit in the drink. The biscuit fell all to

bits and floated about and he tried to hook it out with his finger. Mam was cross: "You'd better get up those stairs, right now!" she said, and was quite surprised when he did just what she said. For the truth was he was looking forward to sleeping in a big single bed of his own. He put his gold belt in the top drawer of the dressing-table. It seemed funny – that belt of his having a whole big drawer to itself.

Then, in his bed near the window, he pulled the blue flowered coverlet up to his chin and fell fast asleep . . . so fast asleep that he didn't even hear the other two coming to bed.

Suddenly he found himself awake, sort of awake without even having to wake up. He was lying there peacefully with his eyes wide open and the room was quite light – even though he seemed to know it was still the middle of the night. Everything was very quiet – except for the sounds of Albert and Humph breathing and snoring.

He began to wonder what had woken him up . . . then his ears pricked up and he felt himself go all strung-up like a tight wire line ready to receive a message.

And that message arrived. It was a soft,

gentle message at first. A sort of slight whimpering message finishing in a very small howl with a growl on the end of it, and it seemed to be right underneath the window. In a flash, Jonny was wide awake. He climbed out of bed and looked through the window. He couldn't see the animal making the noise because it seemed to be tucked well into the wall below . . . And yet he didn't need to see – he knew. "It's Razzle," he whispered. "But how on earth could it have got here?" Then he crept over the deep soft carpet, out of the bedroom to the stairs. The landing was silent and dark, but there was one small light in the hall. As he went down he felt a strange sense of adventure and began to wish he'd put on his gold belt. Then he looked through the glass door out into the porch. Next to the blue pot with the walking sticks in it, sat Razzle. There was a piece of paper tied round his neck with some string.

Jonny stood there not quite knowing what to do next. If he opened the door and went to see what the message said, he was scared that the dog would kick up such a rumpus it would wake the whole place.

But if he tried to take no notice and went straight back to bed, he knew he'd never be able to sleep again for a single second. He would be listening all the time to the little whimpers and whinings down below.

And so he decided to take the plunge. He went towards the front door and at once the dog jumped up and gave a short joyous bark and began wagging its tail madly. Then Jonny discovered an even greater problem: although he could see Razzle and Razzle could see him, there was no way Jonny could open the front door. It was bolted with two large complicated fastenings.

Then he suddenly thought about the window in the television lounge, which was right next to the front porch. Quickly he slipped into the television lounge and went towards the closed curtains. Yes, it was a window with a simple opening like the windows at home. He breathed a sigh of relief as he managed to open it. He climbed out on to the small flower border just underneath it, and felt the friendly, coarse, wiry coat of Razzle brushing against his bare ankles as Razzle rolled about in friendly triumph.

Then he bent down and undid the string round Razzle's neck. It was pink nylon string, and even in the moonlight Jonny recognised it as being some string Rita had had, and he recognised Rita's scrawly writing. Then he frowned . . . what about the dog? After all he couldn't wait outside with it, all night!

The only thing is for it to come inside with *me* instead, he said to himself. And, with his heart almost in his mouth with the terror of being caught, he coaxed the dog upstairs. Then he stroked it and patted it and urged it to go under his bed. At first it didn't want to go, but it disappeared under the bed eventually.

Jonny took the piece of paper which he

was still clutching and smoothed it out. It said: JONNY BRIGGS HIS DOG on it – in typical Rita writing – the sort of writing she did when she was feeling extra mad, all thick and underlined. She must have brought it here last at night. It was just like her to do a thing like that. Then, because everything had gone all quiet again and peaceful – his eyelids began to droop and he fell fast asleep in less than two seconds.

The next thing he knew Albert was nudging him excitedly, and telling him to wake up because there'd been burglars. There was bright sunlight streaming through the curtains. "But they got away without pinching owt," said Albert. "They got in through the television room window, even though the woman swears she shut it last night. She's going to send for the police to come and investigate."

Jonny just lay there in bed and felt himself going all weak at the thought of it all. "How do you know, Albert?" he said. "Won't the police be too busy with special things?"

"What could be more special than this?" said Albert gleefully. "I'm lucky enough to be the first to know because I got up early

to go to the paper shop for some sweets
because I was hungry – and she was up –
and she showed me the place where they
got in through the window. There were all
scuffy marks on the white paint, and all the
flowers outside were trampled on. It looked
as if there'd been a life and death struggle!"

Then Albert hurried out of the bedroom
to tell mam and dad the exciting news.

When he'd gone, Humph said drowsily:
"What was all that in aid of? Have the
Martians landed?"

"It's because the dog's under my bed,"
said Jonny, in a small, miserable voice.

"What?" Humph seemed to come alive
suddenly. He jumped out of his own bed
and came over to Jonny's and bent down

and looked under it. "You're right!" he said, sounding quite amazed. "It's curled up, snoozing its head off. However did it get back here?"

"Our Rita sent it," said Jonny, then he got up and showed Humph the message and told him about how he'd got Razzle in through the window and how it wasn't burglars at all.

They both stood there silently. Even Humph was in a fix – wondering what to do this time to get out of it.

Then he said: "There's one thing that's certain – and that's that we must leave the dog here while we go down for breakfast – and just hope that it won't start making a row. And if we can get through that safely, we won't have a lot more to worry about, because mam and dad'll be paying the bill and we'll be clearing out. So while we're having breakfast, I'll try and think of something." Then Humph shook his head wonderingly: "Trust our Albert to be blowing the whole thing up into a real cops and robbers act!"

About half an hour later a gong sounded. The gong was a sort of shiny brass plate which the lady with the frizzy hair hit with a stick with a leather knob on the end. Jonny asked Mam if he could have a go, but she said "certainly not" straight away.

The Briggs' were all at the same table and there were other people at other tables in the dining-room. And there was one man with a big silvery moustache talking in a loud voice to a lady at another table. "It was a near thing," he said. "They were standing there in the T.V. Lounge with the Silver Tea Set, two diamond necklaces and a hand-painted picture of Captain Cook – when Mrs Lemon herself caught them. She pointed a toy water pistol at them and they fled and left the lot behind. She was a very brave woman. *Very* brave."

There was a murmur of sympathy all round the dining-room.

"The woman with the frizzy hair didn't tell me that," said Albert in a loud, cheery voice. Then he said "Ow" in an even louder voice as Mam kicked him hard under the table with her shoe. And dad said: "Never mind all that – do you want grapefruit juice, porridge or cornflakes?"

Jonny ate his cornflakes slowly. He kept looking at Humph and wondering whether he had thought of anything yet and what he would do if the dog suddenly came rushing into the room barking.

"Hurry up, Jonny," said dad. "Do you want scrambled egg on toast, sausage and tomato, kippers, or plain bacon and eggs?"

"Nothing, thanks."

"Nothing?" hissed mam. "Don't say that! It's a long time till dinner and we'll have to pay for it whether you eat it or not – so you'd better make the most of it."

"And I'll eat it if he doesn't," said Albert quickly, "so you might as well get egg and bacon and pass it on to me."

"Egg and bacon," said Jonny lifelessly, almost beyond himself in his desire to get away from this private hotel horror as quickly as possible before something really awful started.

Then all of a sudden – his worst nightmares started to come true as he heard a sudden lot of fierce barking and a small, scruffy dog came bounding into the dining-room – followed by the lady with frizzy hair. "One of my girls saw this animal run out of a bedroom when she was sorting out the bed linen," she said in a shrill voice with her cheeks all red and angry-looking.

Mam and dad gave each other a quick

horrified look and mam went quite pale.

"I think I know whose it is," said Humph, getting up calmly, and wrinkling his monkey brow which was a sure sign that his brain was working like the clappers. Then he went to the lady and said something. Then he coaxed the dog outside and the lady followed them. Then a few moments later everyone in the dining-room saw the lady going into the hall with an old dog collar and a lead. And a few minutes later the front door opened then closed again . . . and everyone returned to the subject of their breakfasts . . . All except mam, dad and Jonny that is. *They* just sat there helplessly almost as if they were in a dream, while Albert scoffed everything within sight.

Jonny was dreading a terrible row breaking out when mam and dad went to pay the bill after breakfast. He hung about in the background with all the suitcases, trying to imagine what had happened to Humph and Razzle.

Then to his surprise he actually saw the woman with frizzy hair laughing, and he went a bit nearer to find out why. "Yes, it was that poor, scruffy little animal that chased the burglars away," she was saying.

"And although it must be a terrible trial to you, Mrs Briggs, to have a son like that who sleep-walks, it was thanks to him sleep-walking into my lounge that I've now got the true picture of what happened."

"Humphrey? S-sleepwalking?" murmured Mam, amazed. "I don't –"

"Oh yes, mam," said Jonny, before she could say another thing, "I thought you knew . . ."

"Yes," said the woman, beaming at Jonny. "It appears he let the dog rest in the bedroom so as not to cause a disturbance to any of the other guests. And now he's taken him to the police station."

Mam gazed at her in a daze – saying "Mmm," and "yes" and "oh" every few minutes, even though she didn't quite know why. Then they all said goodbye to each other and mam and dad said how comfortable they'd all been.

And just at that moment Humph came back, without the dog. He didn't say anything, but just nodded pleasantly, and helped mam and dad get the suitcases out of the door as quickly as possible.

"That damned dog!" said dad, once they were outside. "Is it going to haunt us for the rest of our lives?"

"Not if he's taken it to the police

station," said mam, smiling thankfully. "I must say it was an awful shock seeing it again – after it disappeared on the train. I thought we'd got rid of it for ever. And when it turned up at Mrs Lemon's Private Hotel I really thought there would be a terrible row over it. And a terrible row would have put me right off trying another weekend. But – all's well that ends well . . ."

Then Jonny saw Humph take a rather deep breath, but he was still calm. He said: "I didn't take it to the police station, mam."

Mam's eyes nearly popped out of her head. "Didn't take it? Whatever do you mean? Don't say you've let it go off on the rampage again! Don't say we're going to have more trouble, with it suddenly turning up and following us just when we don't want it to."

"I didn't take it to the police station because there's no point is there? Suppose they asked me where it'd come from – and I said Middlesbrough. Then they asked me where *I* came from – and *I* said Middlesbrough. If *I* was them, I'd tell us to take it back again on the train after tea, and stop fussing."

Dad groaned like a beaten man. "I expect there's a bit of truth in it," he said. "And I expect that seeing I paid for it to come here, I might as well do the job properly and pay for it to go back as well. Then once it's off that station at the other end it can go to pot as far as I'm concerned – I never want to see it again!" He added grudgingly, "Where is it now then – sitting in someone's Rolls-Royce?"

"I tied it to some railings near the public library," said Humph. "Lots of people leave their dogs there when they're inside looking for library books. I'll go back and fetch him, and Jonny and I'll take him on the beach with us later on in the afternoon while you two go and watch the fishing."

Jonny gave a great gulp of thankfulness. Mam and dad never said another word. They seemed to have caved in completely and had disappeared to find some deckchairs. "We're starting to win, our Jonny," said Humph grinning. "The tide is beginning to turn . . ."

4

"Cooo-eeee!"

At first Jonny took no notice of the call.
He was wearing his new swimming trunks
and there were lots of other people in
swimming trunks, so he thought it must be
meant for someone else further up the
beach. Then the voice called again:
"Jon...neee..."

It was a girl's voice, and when he looked,
he saw Pamela Dean from school standing
there waving to him. She was dressed in a
red-and-white swim-suit with a frill on it
and her hair was all loose and bouncy
looking.

"What are you doing here?" he yelled.

"Come here and I'll tell you," she yelled
back. "I can't come over there because I'm

guarding our Stew's fishing tackle while he goes for some more lugworms."

Jonny went over to her.

"I wasn't sure whether it was this week you were coming to Whitby, or next," she said. "We came for the day in my Uncle Eric's car – and Stew's going to do some fishing. Have you learned to swim yet?"

"Not yet, but I'm going to try and learn – right now – before the tide comes in properly." Then Jonny pointed along the beach: "That's my dad without his shirt on, and that's our mam eating an ice-cream. Our Albert's gone round the Amusements and our Humph's gone to get Razzle a rubber bone to play with."

"Razzle?" said Pam, looking puzzled.

Jonny laughed and said: "Razzle's the name of that stray dog – the one from behind the butcher's at home. It followed us on the train yesterday, and now it's called Razzle."

Pam's eyes grew big and round. "Followed you?" she said. "Whatever did your mam say?"

They both sat on the beach while Jonny told her the whole complicated story. "So now, at last," said Jonny, "it's sorted itself out a bit, and we're taking it back on the train with us after tea."

"And then what will you do?"

"Keep it – if I can," said Jonny proudly. "Humph and I are trying to get it fixed up."

"You lucky thing," said Pam sadly. "My mam won't let us have one."

"My mam doesn't want this one either," said Jonny grinning, "but Humph and I are trying to wear them all down. It would make a good watch-dog. We had four cabbages and a tablecloth off the line pinched not long ago. And if I can keep it, I shall teach it tricks, and how to sing, and train it to count and do sums like they do on the telly."

Then they both began to build a castle with a moat round it for when the tide came right in. And Jonny ran into the sea to practise his swimming with Pam.

It was the first time he had been in that year and even though it was warm and the sun was shining the sea felt quite cold at first. As he waded further and further in, he kept gasping from the cold shock of the water and wondering if he would ever dare to get the whole of himself wet.

Pam didn't go as far in as Jonny, and

splashed about on her tummy letting the waves dash over her and giving little squeals. "Dip your head under," she called. "Once you've got your shoulders wet it won't feel cold any more!"

Jonny took the plunge and bobbed his whole body quickly under the water and gave a big gasp as he jumped up again. After that he stopped feeling cold and started trying to swim properly – using the waves to carry him along.

And then at last – to his amazement and delight – he found he was swimming with *both* feet off the ground. He was so excited that he started to splash and got all muddled up. Then suddenly he found that he couldn't feel the sand under his feet any more . . . the water was much, much deeper and he began to splash about and shout . . . a huge wave came lolloping right over the top of him and took his breath away . . . everything round him seemed to go all blurred and swimmy and he didn't know where he was, or what was happening!

Suddenly he came to. He saw people on the beach, and knew that he must try and get towards them.

He was thinking this and spitting sea-

water out of his mouth and gasping for
breath all at the same time, when he saw a
small, scruffy thing swimming just in front
of him. A drenched, black-and-white tail
was floating on top of the waves . . . It was
so unbelievable it almost seemed like a
dream as Jonny reached forward to grab at
the tail. And then he found himself
swimming again by paddling and splashing
with his back legs.

And the next minute his legs sank back to
the bottom of the sea, and he could stand
up without water washing over the top of
him! And standing there on the sands

smiling were Pamela Dean and Pamela Dean's Uncle Eric and Aunty Sheila, and Jonny's mam and dad, and Albert, and Humph and about ten other people. As he and Razzle came out of the water they began to clap and cheer.

Razzle looked really pleased with himself and jumped about and barked and scampered off again, wagging the long sturdy tail. But Jonny almost crawled out of the water all gaspy and still a bit frightened. He felt as if he had nearly drowned and swum the channel all in one go!

"Very good, lad!" shouted dad, not even coming forward to help him. "You'll make a good little swimmer one of these days."

"What a pity that nuisance of a dog got in your way," shouted mam. "But you did very well, all the same. . . ."

"It didn't get in my way . . ." gasped Jonny indignantly. "That dog saved my life! If it hadn't been for that dog . . ."

And as soon as he said that all the grown-ups seemed to lose interest. They went back to their deckchairs.

"You were quite right, Jonny," said Humph. "It did save your life. It got to you before anyone else realised you needed help. Mam and dad just thought you were larking about. Anyway, it's taught you a lesson! *Never* go too far out or get out of your depth."

Jonny nodded. Then he grinned and said: "Well, at least I can swim." And he ran back into the water again with Pam. But this time he didn't go so far out. And they both found they could beat the Brown brothers any day, when it came to proper swimming.

"And that dog can beat them any day when it comes to proper life-saving," said Jonny happily.

After tea, when Jonny had said goodbye to Pam, and when the Briggs family – complete with Razzle in a collar and lead – had got itself on the train going back to Middlesbrough, Jonny said to Humph: "It seems to have worked – dad bought that ticket for Razzle and never said a word, and mam even gave it a chocolate drop and forgot to give Albert one. And just look how good it's being, as quiet as anything – and really clean-looking."

Humph smiled. But he didn't say much. As far as he was concerned, the struggle was over for the time being. Though there was

one thing that Humph knew . . . *He* knew
that a good little dog sitting next to them
on the train wasn't quite the same thing as
a dog at home in Port Street – with three
girls – including Rita the trouble stirrer,
plus three boys and mam and dad.

Then he grinned to himself silently and
forgot it all because his book was good –
and it was no use worrying about all *that* till
the time actually arrived – especially as
their Jonny was so happy!

But the beautiful happiness on the train
was a bit like the weather when the sun
suddenly decides to go in. . . . As soon as
they were off the train and near home
again, mam began to chunter, "I don't
know what we're going to do with that
blessed dog," she groaned. "And as far as
food is concerned, there won't be a thing in
the house for it! I hope our Sandra
remembered the extra bread and milk and
there's plenty of hot water when we get
back. A cup of tea's what I could do with,
just at this moment. A nice cup of tea in my
own kitchen. A cup of tea's never the same
anywhere else."

Then she caught sight of the dog trotting
along by the side of them, and she looked at

Jonny. It was a sort of undecided look, and Jonny gazed back at her, his heart thumping a little harder than usual. He hoped with all his hope that she would suddenly smile and say: "All right Jonny, I give in. Razzle is one of the family now."

Instead, it was just the opposite. Mam suddenly gave a determined sigh and the little bits of sunburn on her forehead and her nose all creased up as she said sharply: "As soon as we set foot in the door of our house, Jonny, you can take that animal round to the back of the butcher's where it belongs, otherwise I can't see myself enjoying a peaceful cup of tea in my own kitchen ever again."

Jonny felt as if someone had poured a jug of icy water on him. He looked round desperately, hoping for at least some cries of support, but no one said a word. And even dad said: "Well – I expect it's best in the long run. All I can say is, it isn't every stray dog in the country as gets a paid holiday weekend at the seaside. Quite honestly I was getting used to it, though. There's a chap at work who's got a huge dog kennel he wants to get rid of. It would probably have fitted in our backyard . . . if we'd been driven to it. . . ."

"We're not having anything else stuck in that backyard," said mam. "And that's final."

Sandra was all smiles when they got in. She and Pat had got the house looking cleaner and neater than Jonny had ever seen it. Mam's face positively glowed with happiness at the sight, as she went round inspecting things – just as if she'd been away for two years – instead of two days!

She kept saying things like: "I see you've tidied all those magazines away then – *and* cleaned out the cupboard! What *good* girls you are . . ."

And all the Briggs females smiled at each other in contented, co-operative bliss.

But Sandra's smile slackened a bit when there was a whimpering sound at the front door. Like magic she looked straight at Jonny. For a second, he nearly hung his head and looked down at his toes as if he was ashamed of something. Then he didn't! He suddenly thought, *why should I?* So he stared her out.

"Not that dog *again?*" she said, smiling exasperatedly.

Jonny nodded, and before he could reply,

mam said: "But not for long, Sandra love.
Our Jonny's taking it back to where it came
from — round the back of those shops – right
NOW!" Then mam gave Jonny one of the
looks he hated most. It was one of her
sarcastic *you're not going to get the better of me
Sunny Jim* looks. It was a glare with a jerk of
the head, and a jerk of her thumb backwards
at the same time telling him to BEAT IT! It
was the final ultimatum.

Miserably he walked to the front door to
find Razzle and take him back. The dog was
still there, and when Jonny reached it it
jumped up and wagged its tail excitedly.

Slowly, Jonny picked up its dangling lead,
and together he and Razzle trailed down
Port Street.

It was at this moment that he saw Rita

arriving back home with Mavis, all loaded with suitcases and big paper bags and soft cuddly toys won on the amusement stalls.

Jonny groaned. He hadn't thought anything could get worse. But seeing Rita right now was about the last straw, and he tried to see if there was anywhere he could hide away till she'd walked past. But it was no use, he was due for a head-on collision. He felt as if he and Razzle were leading a whole regiment of soldiers to face a marauding and vicious army.

He stuck his chin high in the air and walked fast . . . and forward . . . closer and closer . . . with Razzle trotting obediently by his side. He imagined the final onslaught. The yellings and howls of the enemy, the tearing of huge paper bags in a battle to the death; the kicking of shins – the devastation such as Port Street had never seen before in the whole of its history!

Then: "Hello, our Jonny! Did you have a nice time then?" said Rita.

Mavis said, "Rita and I had a marvellous time – didn't we?"

Then Rita looked down at the dog and said: "I see you got the dog back safely . . ."

Jonny just couldn't get over it. He stood

there dumbfounded.

Then Rita said the most amazing thing –
quite out of the blue. She said: "It's a very
good jumper is that dog. It can run at a
terrific speed and it can fly through the air
over a four-foot wire fence with the ease of a
racehorse, can't it, Mavis?" And Mavis
nodded solemnly at Rita.

"In fact," said Rita, tossing her fair, sun-
bleached hair triumphantly, "these two boy
friends we met from Billy Boskett's circus,
told us we were fools to have dumped it
back on you. They saw it chasing this rabbit
– and they were astounded – weren't they
Mavis?"

Mavis nodded again. Then she went a bit
pink and said: "Mine – the one with the
curly hair and deep blue eyes – was the one
who was astounded most. If we'd been
staying longer, they wanted us to get the
dog back and they'd have helped us to train
it to be a circus star."

"Yes," said Rita thoughtfully, "I think
the circus ones were a bit more fun than the
Dracula ones. We could always write and
tell them how the dog's getting on. Then
perhaps they'd take a trip over here to see
it, or invite us back to see them . . ."

At last, Jonny got his voice back. "You won't be able to," he said. "Because our mam says it's to go back to being a stray dog behind the back of the butcher's."

Rita's face fell a mile. "A stray dog?" she said in a pained, shocked voice, as if she'd never heard of such a thing in her life before. "Fancy our mam being as cruel as all that! People aren't supposed to fill the world with stray dogs! In fact I wouldn't be a bit surprised if there wasn't a law against people turning dogs out on to the streets as strays. Our mam could probably be fined for it. And being fined would be far more expensive than getting a dog-licence for it."

Jonny brightened up. For once in his life he completely agreed with their Rita. "P'raps I'd better not take it back to behind the shops, then," he said. "I don't want our mam getting into trouble. Hadn't you better tell her about getting fined, when you get back in, our Rita?"

Rita nodded. Then she and Mavis started to walk towards home again with Jonny a few yards behind them with the dog.

"You'd better not come in this time, Mavis," Rita was saying, "because you know what dad is about people draping themselves about. But thanks for helping to carry all the parcels and I'll see you tomorrow at seven and let you know what happened. I'll give mam and dad the presents first and get our Jonny to shuffle off to the park for a bit with the animal. That'll give me time to get it all sorted out." Then she turned round to Jonny and said, "Take it to the park, and don't come back for at least an hour."

Jonny almost flew to the park. He knew the battle was over. He knew that once the enemy was on his side, mam and dad were gonners! Rita was a sure sign of their downfall. He whooped as he ran in the park gates and two ladies frowned slightly. Then, when he got to the big broad stretch of grass in Albert Park, he let Razzle off the lead and they both raced each other. Then he tried stretching out his arms, and Razzle jumped over it as easy as wink. Then he said "*Stop*" to Razzle, and Razzle stood still. And he said "*Go*", and Razzle moved and wagged his tail and jumped about again. It was as if he had already been trained by someone else at some time.

Mam was pleasantly surprised to see Rita arriving home at a respectable hour, and on

her own and looking so well and good-
humoured. They both kissed each other
affectionately, and Rita gave dad a big hug
and told him she had brought him and
mam some nice presents.

"Thank you very much love," said dad as
he stared at a purple tie with *Me for Boss*
written on it in white. "I'm sure the lads at
work will appreciate that – even if no one
else does . . ." Then he hastily wrapped it
up again and disappeared.

Meanwhile, mam was gazing at an apron in bright pink which said *I'm the one who does all the work round here*, also in white writing, and murmuring, "Rita you shouldn't have!" But she was thinking to herself that people wouldn't need aprons like that if everyone did their fair share. Then she folded it up and pretended to be absolutely delighted while Albert shouted: "What about the rest of us then? Didn't you even bring us any rock back?"

"You? When you've only just got back yourself? Did you bring *me* anything?" And Albert disappeared as well.

Then Rita gave Pat and Sandra a bottle of scent each and Humph a giant humbug because she knew it was safest to keep in his good books. Then she said to mam: "By the way, our mam – I just saw our Jonny when I was coming home and he was nearly in the most serious trouble . . ."

"Trouble!" gasped mam, almost shivering as if she had become allergic to the word. "Don't say that, our Rita. Don't say he's in trouble the very second he's back home!"

"He had this dog with him," said Rita. "And you can thank your lucky stars that I was there to step in and save him before the police came . . ."

"Police?" said mam, quivering anxiously. "Surely not . . . after all he's not very old . . . he's not *wilfully* bad . . . it's just that he doesn't always think."

"Well, he was thinking well enough this time, our mam . . . And *do you know* what he was doing?" Rita waited dramatically for the suspense to mount. . . .

"No? What was it? What was he up to?"

"He was making this dog into a stray dog! He was letting it off its lead and just leaving it to wander the streets! And you know as well as I do that *that* is against the law. I know it for a fact from Wally who's in the police force."

"Oh," said mam, weakly. "So what did you do?"

"What could I do? I just told this man he was mistaken. I said, 'Excuse me but this is my little brother and this is *our* dog. It isn't a stray at all – it's just that my brother is letting it off its lead in the wrong place.' Then, in front of this man, I told our Jonny to take it to the park."

"Oh," said mam again. Then she said: "Does that mean that everything's all right again?"

"It does – if we keep the dog and say it's ours from now on," said Rita ruthlessly.

Mam gave a big sigh. "Oh," she said for the third time.

Then Rita said casually: "Actually it's quite a clever dog, our mam. It's very good at jumping. It's almost like a circus dog . . ." Then she went away.

Jonny came back an hour later, with Razzle on the lead. He came in quietly round the back, into the yard – hardly daring to think what might happen.

And as he came through the open yard door – he saw mam and dad standing outside. And dad was saying: "Well, if we put that kennel *there* it wouldn't be in the way of the cabbages."

And mam was saying: "Well, perhaps you're right."

Then they both turned and looked at Jonny and Razzle and smiled slightly as if they still weren't quite on earth but couldn't do much about it.

"What's it called then?" said dad, grinning very slightly at Jonny as if he didn't want mam to see.

"Razzle," said Jonny, grinning back and feeling his spirits soaring again and thinking how great life was!

"Razzle – is it . . .?" said mam looking at it again and shaking her head. Then she said: "All right then, you've won. And if it causes any trouble at all for one single second it will have to be officially and painlessly disposed of. I for one have no intention of being led a dog's life on top of the one we've already got!"

And Jonny said: "Yes, mam, no, mam!" as eagerly as if she was a Company Sergeant Major, and dashed off again with Razzle.

And when he got back to school on Monday and told Pamela Dean all about it, they both agreed it was the best weekend that anyone could have had in the whole of their lives!

More Jonny Briggs titles available from BBC/Knight Books

☐ 33118 6	Jonny Briggs	£1.25
☐ 27532 4	Jonny Briggs and the Great Razzle Dazzle	£1.25
☐ 28042 5	Jonny Briggs and the Giant Cave	95p
☐ 33028 8	Jonny Briggs and the Galloping Wedding	£1.25
☐ 34837 2	Jonny Briggs and the Jubilee Concert	£1.25
☐ 35338 4	Jonny Briggs and the Ghost	£1.25

Also available from BBC/Knight Books:

JOAN AIKEN

☐ 35339 2   Arabel and the escaped Black Mamba   £1.25

All these books are available at your local bookshop or newsagent, or can be ordered direct from the publisher. Just tick the titles you want and fill in the form below.

Prices and availability subject to change without notice.

KNIGHT BOOKS, P.O. Box 11, Falmouth, Cornwall.

Please send cheque or postal order, and allow the following for postage and packing:

U.K. – 55p for one book, plus 22p for the second book, and 14p for each additional book ordered up to a £1.75 maximum.

B.F.P.O. & EIRE – 55p for the first book, plus 22p for the second book, and 14p per copy for the next 7 books, 8p per book thereafter.

OTHER OVERSEAS CUSTOMERS – £1.00 for the first book, plus 25p per copy for each additional book.

Name .....PAUL NIOI...

Address .....22 Hermitage Green...............
Glenrothes FIFE